marla frazee

THE FARMER AND THE CLOWN

Beach Lane Books

NEW YORK · LONDON · TORONTO · SYDNEY · NEW DELHI

For the troupe that is my family

BEACH LANE BOOKS
An imprint of Simon & Schuster Children's Publishing Division
1230 Avenue of the Americas, New York, New York 10020
Copyright © 2014 by Marla Frazee
All rights reserved, including the right of reproduction in whole or
in part in any form.
BEACH LANE BOOKS is a trademark of Simon & Schuster, Inc.
For information about special discounts for bulk purchases, please
contact Simon & Schuster Special Sales at 1-866-506-1949 or
business@simonandschuster.com.
The Simon & Schuster Speakers Bureau can bring authors to your
live event. For more information or to book an event, contact the
Simon & Schuster Speakers Bureau at 1-866-248-3049 or visit
our website at www.simonspeakers.com.
Book design by Marla Frazee and Ann Bobco
The illustrations for this book are rendered in black Prismacolor
pencil and gouache.
Manufactured in China
0714 SCP

10 9 8 7 6 5 4 3 2
Library of Congress Cataloging-in-Publication Data
Frazee, Marla, author, illustrator.
The farmer and the clown / Marla Frazee. — First edition.
pages cm
Summary: A wordless picture book in which a farmer rescues a baby
clown who has bounced off the circus train, and reunites him with
his clown family.
ISBN 978-1-4424-9744-3 (hardcover) —
ISBN 978-1-4424-9745-0 (ebook)
[1. Farmers—Fiction. 2. Clowns—Fiction. 3. Circus—Fiction.
4. Stories without words.] I. Title.
PZ7.F866Far 2014
[E]—dc23
2013019361

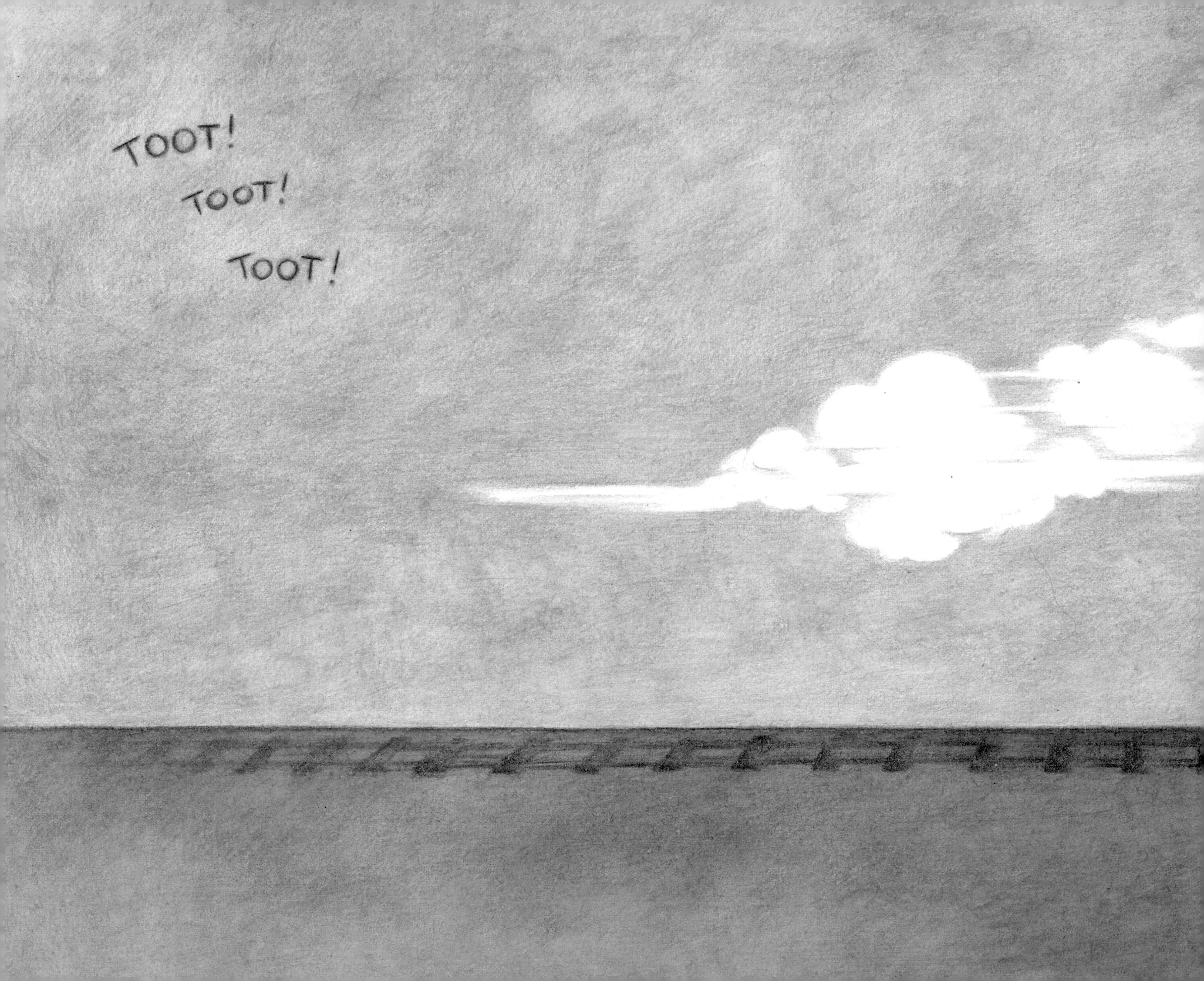
TOOT!
TOOT!
TOOT!